our
Environment

Acid Rain

Peggy J. Parks

KIDHAVEN PRESS
An imprint of Thomson Gale, a part of The Thomson Corporation

THOMSON
—— ✦ ——
GALE

Detroit • New York • San Francisco • San Diego • New Haven, Conn.
Waterville, Maine • London • Munich

For more information, contact
KidHaven Press
27500 Drake Rd.
Farmington Hills, MI 48331-3535
Or you can visit our Internet site at http://www.gale.com

LIBRARY OF CONGRESS CATALOGING-IN-PUBLICATION DATA

Parks, Peggy J., 1951–
   Acid rain / by Peggy J. Parks.
      p. cm. — (Our environment)
   Includes bibliographical references and index.
   ISBN 0-7377-2628-8 (hard cover : alk. paper)
   1. Acid rain—Environmental aspects—Juvenile literature. I. Title. II. Series.
   TD195.44.P37 2005
   363.738'6—dc22

                                                                    2005012461

Printed in the United States of America

contents

chapter one

Poisoned Precipitation

Rain is good for the Earth. It causes grass to turn green and beautifully colored flowers to bloom. It soaks farmland so crops can grow and seeps deep into the ground to water the roots of thirsty trees. Rain replenishes lakes, rivers, and streams. It naturally cleanses the land and washes the leaves of trees and plants. Without rain, the planet would be a barren place where living things could not survive. Not all rain is the same, however. In some areas of the world, it is polluted with acids. When this rain falls from the sky, it looks exactly like normal rain—but it is not normal at all. It is acid rain, and it can damage the environment.

What Is Acid Rain?

The term *acid rain* applies to more than just rain. It is used to describe any precipitation with an acid content (or acidity) that is higher than normal. Snow, sleet, hail, and even morning dew can contain acids. Acid particles can also cling to fog, and because fog is wetter than rain, acid fog can be the most damaging precipitation of all. Science author Michael Allaby tells why: "Fog droplets are much smaller and remain in the air. Because the fog is not falling, it envelops objects exposed to it, allowing droplets to coat all surfaces."[1]

A red-eyed tree frog in the South American rain forest sits on a bromeliad flower during a heavy shower.

Acids in the atmosphere are not always wet. They can also exist in a dry form. They cling to gases and dust fragments in the air. This is especially true in dry climates or in places where droughts are common.

Acid rain lands on all types of surfaces, including trees, buildings, cars, homes, and bridges. It can be blown in the wind and travel hundreds of miles (km) away from its original source. It also finds its way into lakes, streams, and rivers. When

A scientist tests the pH level of a New York lake that has been dramatically affected by acid rain.

this happens, the water can become too **acidic**. This happened to Little Echo Pond, a lake located in northeastern New York. Because of acid rain pollution, it is now one of the most acidic lakes in the United States. Fish and other organisms that live in the water are not used to high acid levels. If the acid level continues to rise, they could die.

Measuring Acid Rain

Scientists study acid rain by collecting samples of rainwater. Working in laboratories or out in the field, they test the water with special instruments called **pH** meters. Acid levels are measured according to a pH scale, which ranges in number from 0 to 14. Substances with low pH numbers have the highest acid content. For instance, battery acid is strong enough to burn holes in clothing and it has a pH of less than 1. Some other acidic substances are lemon juice, vinegar, and carbonated soft drinks. One of the strongest acids is found in the human stomach. It measures between 1 and 2 on the pH scale. That is 1 million times more acidic than pure water!

On the opposite end of the scale are the low-acid substances, which have a high pH. These are known as **alkalis** or bases. Examples include baking soda and soapy water. Just because a substance is an alkali does not mean it is mild or harmless. With a pH of 14, drain cleaner is one of the most alkaline substances. It is extremely strong and can burn as badly as acid can. The ideal pH is neither acidic nor alkaline. For instance, distilled water (water with no impurities) has a pH of 7, which is considered neutral.

Rain and Nature

Normal rain is more acidic than distilled water because of natural acids present in the atmosphere. The average pH of unpolluted rain is about 5.6. When the pH measures lower than that, scientists consider it a probable sign of acid rain. This can vary widely from region to region. For instance, in the eastern part of Canada some rain is as acidic as lemon juice or vinegar. In the western part of the country, acid levels are much lower.

When rain is of normal acidity, natural alkaline chemicals can help keep the pH in balance. These chemicals are present in Earth's rocks and soils. They are also found in many lakes, especially those that have limestone bottoms instead of rock. The natural alkalis mix with the acids, which buffers them by reducing their strength. This is nature's way of keeping the environment in balance. However, when precipitation is highly acidic (with a pH below 5.6), the natural alkalis can be destroyed. They can no longer balance the pH, which causes acid levels to rise over time.

Discovery of Acid Rain

The first scientist to closely study acid levels was Robert Angus Smith. Originally from Scotland, Smith

The pH Scale

The pH scale measures how acidic an object is. Acids have pH values under 7 and bases (also called alkalis) have pH values over 7. If a substance has a pH value of 7 it is called neutral, and is neither an acid or a base.

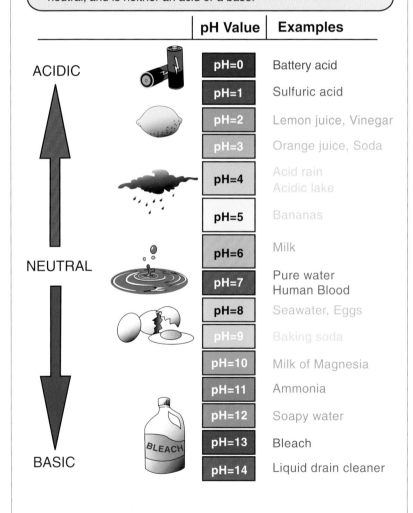

	pH Value	Examples
ACIDIC	pH=0	Battery acid
	pH=1	Sulfuric acid
	pH=2	Lemon juice, Vinegar
	pH=3	Orange juice, Soda
	pH=4	Acid rain / Acidic lake
	pH=5	Bananas
	pH=6	Milk
NEUTRAL	pH=7	Pure water / Human Blood
	pH=8	Seawater, Eggs
	pH=9	Baking soda
	pH=10	Milk of Magnesia
	pH=11	Ammonia
	pH=12	Soapy water
	pH=13	Bleach
BASIC	pH=14	Liquid drain cleaner

In this 1912 photo, workers shovel coal into boilers in a factory in Manchester, England. Burning coal releases pollutants that create acid rain.

moved to Manchester, England, where he worked as a chemist. In the mid-1800s, he became concerned about air pollution in Manchester. This was during the Industrial Revolution, when industry grew more rapidly than in any other period in history. Manchester was a major manufacturing city, as Allaby describes: "Mills and factories sprang up everywhere in the burgeoning city, and, because the whole industry was powered by steam that was raised by burning coal, all the mills and factories had tall chimney stacks that poured forth smoke, steam, waste gases, textile fibers, and dust."[2]

The thick smoke that constantly hovered in the Manchester air worried Smith. He decided to study the pollution by analyzing water samples. He collected rainwater and melted snow from areas in and around the city. Then he examined the samples in his laboratory. He observed that the water contained very high levels of acid. This was also the case in areas downwind from Manchester. That meant toxic smoke was traveling in the wind. In areas far away from the city, however, acid levels were much lower. Smith concluded that acid rain was caused by pollution from the factories. He did not know exactly how or why this occurred, but he was sure he was right.

Smith made his findings public in 1852. Twenty years later he wrote a book entitled *Air and Rain: The Beginnings of a Chemical Climatology*. Following the book's release, other scientists began to monitor rainfall acidity in areas throughout Europe. However, Smith's theories were not widely accepted in the scientific world. It was not until the next century that people began to see just how damaging acid rain could be.

chapter two

Acids in the Clouds

More than 150 years have passed since Smith began studying acid rain. In that time, scientists have gained a lot of knowledge about it. They are still not quite sure how the acids form. What they do know is that the process starts with certain atmospheric gases. When these gases come in contact with water, oxygen, and sunlight, a chemical reaction takes place. This changes the gases into acids.

From Carbon to Acid

Smith's research focused on pollution caused by humans. Modern scientists now know that nature also contributes to acids in the atmosphere. One plentiful atmospheric gas is **carbon dioxide**, or CO_2. This gas is created whenever animals, includ-

Stripped of all their leaves, these trees in a forest in North Carolina are victims of acid rain.

ing humans, breathe. CO_2 also forms when living things die and their bodies decompose, or break down. The carbon that has been stored inside their bodies is released into the soil, where it reacts with oxygen. The carbon changes into CO_2, which escapes into the atmosphere.

Whenever CO_2 comes into contact with water —including the water droplets that make up clouds —it dissolves. This reaction causes the formation of mild carbonic acid. This natural acid remains in the atmosphere and affects precipitation, as Michael Allaby explains: "Because carbon dioxide is distributed evenly throughout the lower atmosphere, every cloud encounters it and so every cloud contains dissolved carbon dioxide and is slightly acidic. This means that water falling from the cloud as hail, snow, or rain is also acid, as are fog, dew, and frost. . . . That is its natural condition."[3]

The Role of Volcanoes

Another gas in the atmosphere is **sulfur dioxide.** Nature sends this gas into the air whenever a volcano erupts. During violent eruptions, millions of tons (metric tons) of the gas are blasted into the sky. As with CO_2, sulfur dioxide undergoes a chemical reaction in the atmosphere to form sulfuric acid. However, it is much stronger and more harmful than the carbonic acid created by CO_2.

In Hawaii, acid rain caused by volcanoes is an ongoing problem. Volcanoes erupt frequently, and the sulfuric acid mixes with fog to form what Hawaiians call "vog." It is highly acidic—nearly as strong as battery acid. When vog lands on plants, it can destroy them by burning the leaves. Farmers have even suffered losses to crops grown in greenhouses because the acidic mist squeezes through air vents.

There are also health risks associated with vog. When vog is especially thick, the air becomes dangerous to breathe. Drinking water is affected by

A fountain of lava spews into the air as molten lava pours out of the crater of Hawaii's Kilauea volcano.

the toxic fog as well. Many Hawaiians depend on rainwater for drinking. They collect it in rooftop structures known as catchment systems. When the acid rain falls on roofs, it can eat away the lead from roofing nails and paint. The contaminated rainwater then enters the catchment system and makes the water poisonous to drink.

The Human Contribution

In spite of nature's contribution to acid rain, humans bear much of the blame. Most atmospheric acids are created by the burning of fossil fuels: coal, oil, and natural gas. These fuels are used by people all over the world. When they are burned, they emit sulfur dioxide and **nitrogen oxide**. These human-made gases turn into acids in the same way that natural gases do. The difference is, humans release far more of these pollutants into the atmosphere than nature does—billions of tons (metric tons) every year. The result is precipitation with a far greater acid content than nature creates on its own.

Most of the sulfuric acid in the atmosphere is caused by the burning of coal. This fuel was dis-covered thousands of years ago, but during the Industrial Revolution its use began to soar. Factories throughout Europe burned coal to fuel steam engines. Ships and railroad trains burned it to power their steam boilers. When the Industrial Revolution spread to North America, factories sprang up all over the United States. Cotton mills were powered by coal, and weapons factories burned coal in huge iron furnaces. By the early 19th century, coal was being used to produce electricity.

Pollution from Power

The demand for electricity has skyrocketed over the years, and the demand for coal has grown along with it. Today coal is mainly used to create elec-

To generate electricity, power plants around the world burn coal, which releases sulfuric acid into the atmosphere.

tricity. At power plants it is used to heat water to high temperatures to form steam. The steam moves large turbines that make electrical power. Coal is used to generate about 40 percent of the world's total electricity. In the United States, more than half of all electrical plants burn coal. According to a

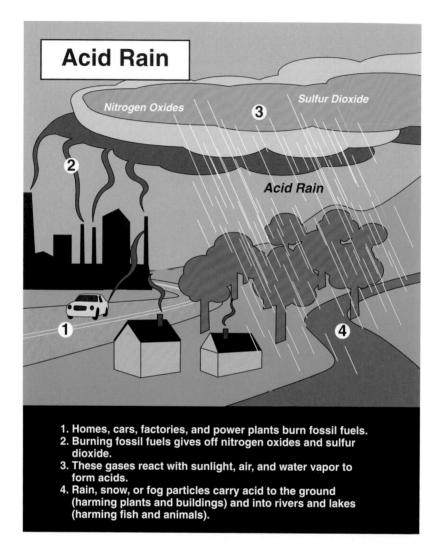

Acid Rain

Nitrogen Oxides   3   Sulfur Dioxide

Acid Rain

1. Homes, cars, factories, and power plants burn fossil fuels.
2. Burning fossil fuels gives off nitrogen oxides and sulfur dioxide.
3. These gases react with sunlight, air, and water vapor to form acids.
4. Rain, snow, or fog particles carry acid to the ground (harming plants and buildings) and into rivers and lakes (harming fish and animals).

2004 report by the Environmental Protection Agency, electric-power generation is responsible for nearly 70 percent of all sulfur dioxide emissions nationwide.

The Worldwatch Institute says that one coal-burning power plant can release 30,000 tons (27,215 metric tons) of sulfur dioxide in a year. Such plants often have tall smokestacks to vent the emissions high into the air. This can help curb pollution in cities, but it also means that the pollution can be blown long distances by the wind. In the New York State Lakes Web site author John V. Miller explains: "Emissions [travel easily] when they are spewed from giant smokestacks into the prevailing winds. In the U.S. there are 179 industrial smokestacks measuring from 500 to 1000 feet [152 to 304m] high."[4]

Another gas emitted by electrical power plants is nitrogen oxide. It forms whenever oil and gas are burned. Of the 25 million tons (23 million metric tons) of nitrogen oxide discharged in the United States each year, about 21 percent is made by power plants. The gas also escapes through chimneys when people burn fuels in furnaces. However, the greatest amount of nitrogen oxide in the atmosphere by far comes from transportation. Automobiles, trucks, buses, trains, and other vehicles burn gasoline and other fuels. Nitrogen oxide is then emitted through their exhaust systems. No matter where it comes from, nitrogen oxide in the atmosphere can change into nitric acid.

Studying the Past

Through the years scientists have learned about atmospheric acids in various ways. For instance, they have studied massive glaciers found in Antarctica and the Arctic Circle. These ice formations took hundreds of thousands of years to form. As

By studying diatoms (seen here magnified) in sediment layers, scientists can determine how pH levels have changed over time.

precipitation continued to pile up, layers of ice formed and were squeezed tightly together. Within these layers lie clues about the atmospheric conditions throughout history. By gathering samples, scientists can analyze the layers to see how the ice has changed over time. They have found that the atmosphere has grown more acidic over the past 150 years. Before the Industrial Revolution, the pH of the glacial ice was about 6. Since then it has dropped to between 4 and 4.5.

Scientists also learn about acids by studying organisms known as **diatoms**. These members of the algae family live in bodies of water. Over the years, diatoms have died and decomposed. Their remains have been deposited in layers of sediment on the bottoms of lakes and streams. The organisms thrive only at certain pH levels. By studying the layers of sediment, scientists can see whether or not diatoms were present at a particular time. From this they can determine how the pH of the water has changed over the years.

Research has come a long way since acid rain was first discovered in the 1800s. However, there are still questions about how and why it forms. Scientists know it starts with gases such as sulfur dioxide and nitrogen oxide. They also know that some chemical reaction takes place that changes the gases into acids. As research methods improve the mysteries of acid rain may someday be solved.

chapter three

Effects of Acid Rain

As serious as acid rain can be, some areas of the world are not affected by it. Australia, for instance, is a large country, but its population is relatively small. This means fewer vehicles pollute the air with nitrogen oxide emissions. Because oceans surround Australia, masses of polluted air do not blow over from other countries. Also, the coal that Australians use has a low sulfur content. When this coal is burned, much less sulfur dioxide is created.

Some Problem Spots

China, on the other hand, has one of the worst acid rain problems in the world. More than a billion people live in China, and that number grows by about 14 million each year. With so many peo-

Tourists marvel at the giant Buddha statue in Leshan, China. Sadly, acid rain from pollution is damaging the ancient monument.

ple, an enormous number of vehicles travel the roads. This is not the main cause of atmospheric gases, though. The biggest cause is high-sulfur coal burned in power plants. China relies on coal for most of its energy. The power plants use old, out-dated technology, so they must burn millions of tons (metric tons) of extra coal. As a result, China is the world's largest source of sulfur dioxide emissions. Environmental official Wang Jian explains the severity of the problem: "The regional acid rain pollution is still out of control and even worse in some southern cities."[5]

Acid rain has also caused serious damage in the northeastern part of the United States. This is mostly due to coal-burning power and industrial plants in the Midwest. These plants have tall smokestacks that vent emissions high into the atmosphere. Prevailing winds blow from west to east and carry sulfur dioxide along with them. This pollution does not stop at U.S. borders. Scientists estimate that the United States is responsible for about half of Canada's acid rain.

Forests at Risk

In eastern Canada and the northeastern United States, acid rain causes severe damage to forests. For instance, maple syrup producers in New Hampshire and Vermont, as well as in some areas of Canada, have lost many sugar maple trees due to acid damage. In Pennsylvania, trees that once turned vivid shades of crimson and gold in the autumn no longer change color. In New York's Adirondack region, acid rain has killed more than half of the red spruce trees.

Trees at high elevations are at greatest risk, as tall pines are bathed in acid clouds. On the highest ridges of the Appalachian Mountains, this has led to the decline of spruce forests. The same thing has happened in Germany's Black Forest. Over the years, acid rain has seriously harmed the trees. Howard Perlman of the U.S. Geological Survey visited the forest and describes how it looked: "Much of the Black Forest was indeed black because so much of the green pine needles had been destroyed, leaving only the black trunks and limbs!"[6]

Sugar maple trees throughout New England are being lost to acid rain.

The damage from acid rain is a slow process that often begins at the ground level. The acids strip valuable nutrients such as calcium and magnesium from the soil. The nutrients are then washed away before the trees and plants can use them to grow. Also, just as acid can burn skin, highly acidic rain can burn the leaves and needles of trees. It eats holes in the waxy coating, leaving dead brown spots. If too many of these spots form, trees can lose their ability to create food through a process known as photosynthesis. The trees become weakened, which makes them more vulnerable to disease, insect infestations, drought, and frost.

Effect on Lakes

Acid rain can also harm lakes by lowering the pH of the water. As the lake becomes more acidic, creatures living there can no longer survive. The lake becomes known as a dead lake. To the casual observer, dead lakes can look beautiful because the water is crystal clear. But the clear water is actually a sign that everything that once lived in the lake has died.

To examine the effects of acid rain on lakes, scientists performed a study on Wisconsin's Little Rock Lake beginning in 1984. The lake is shaped like an hourglass, and scientists used a mesh curtain to divide it in half. They kept one side of the lake in its natural state. Over a period of six years, they intentionally polluted the other half with acid. As

A scientist catches a trout as part of a study to determine the effects of acid rain on the fish populations of a New York lake.

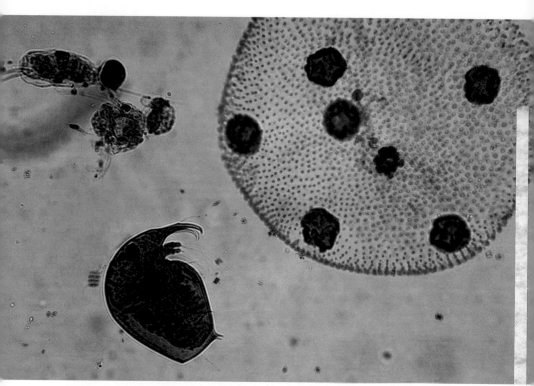

This is a highly magnified image of zooplankton, microscopic organisms that are an important part of the aquatic food chain.

the water's pH decreased, the scientists closely observed the changes that occurred.

Some fish in the lake, such as bass and perch, survived the acidic water. However, most organisms —including the offspring of the fish—did not survive. There were also radical changes in microscopic organisms known as **zooplankton**, which provide food for other aquatic creatures. Some rare species thrived and began to dominate the lake. Other species vanished entirely. As more and more of the lake's creatures died, the water became as clear as glass. Then mosslike algae began to spread across the lake bottom. It became so thick that it choked out all plant life, and scientists nicknamed it "elephant snot."

In 1990 the scientists stopped adding acid to the water. Gradually the lake began returning to its normal state. This was good news, because it meant the lake had the ability to naturally heal itself. The scientists learned, however, that the healing was a slow process that took many years. Although Little Rock Lake is much the same today as it was before the experiment, some species that lived there were completely wiped out. Scientists do not know if they will ever return.

Damage to Structures

Most people are aware of acid rain's effects on forests and lakes. What is not so widely known is how it can damage some structures. This is especially true with ancient buildings and monuments that are made of limestone, marble, and other types of stone. The acids eat away at the material and gradually dissolve it. Some of this weathering is normal, even when rain is unpolluted. When rain is acidic, however, the process happens much faster. One example is the world-famous Taj Mahal in India, which is slowly being destroyed by acid rain. Writer Jim Motavalli describes the damage: "Over recent decades, tourists have watched the Taj Mahal's marble facade fade from dazzling

A car is pulled out of the Ohio River after the collapse of the Silver Bridge in 1967.

white to dingy yellow, and its dome begin flaking away under a relentless attack by acid rain."[7]

Acid rain can destroy metal as well as stone. One tragic example of this occurred in December 1967. The Silver Bridge, which crossed the Ohio River, buckled and collapsed during rush hour traffic. Thirty-one vehicles and more than 60 people were thrown into the water, and 46 people died. Following the accident, engineers reconstructed the bridge piece by piece. They spent two years studying it and finally determined what had happened. A single metal joint had broken, which led to a chain reaction. One by one, joints continued breaking until the bridge snapped in half. The first joint had broken because of a tiny flaw in the metal, which was further weakened by years of acid pollution from nearby factories.

Although acid rain is not a problem everywhere in the world, there are areas where it has caused serious damage. Forests and lakes have been harmed by it, as have structures such as buildings, monuments, and bridges. Research has shown that the natural environment can heal itself, even after being polluted by acid rain. However, that can only happen if scientists find a way to stop it.

chapter four

Can Acid Rain Be Stopped?

Acid rain is not a problem worldwide. Where acid rain does exist, however, scientists and others search for ways of stopping it. They are also looking for ways to fix the damage that has already been done.

The Cost of Cleaning Up

The damage caused by acid rain did not happen overnight, and neither can it be erased overnight. Trying to stop pollution from sulfur dioxide and nitrogen oxide is an enormous challenge. The gases are largely caused by burning fossil fuels, and people all over the world depend on these fuels every day. Coal, oil, and natural gas are used for everything from creating electricity to keeping automobiles running. New York University professor

Attempting to control lake acidity, scientists in Sweden spray tons of agricultural lime into waterway systems.

Martin Hoffert explains their importance: "Fossil fuels have been a great boon to our civilization. Without them, we would never have had the Industrial Revolution, we would never have made the incredible progress that's happened over the past two hundred years, and we would still be living the way people did in the Middle Ages."[8]

Environmental Legislation

Scientists and legislators know that fossil fuels are essential to people's way of life. That is why it is such a challenge to lessen their use. However,

Under President Bush's Clear Skies Initiative, coal-fired power plants must reduce their sulfur dioxide and nitrogen oxide emissions by 2018.

most recognize that acid rain is a problem that must be addressed.

In the United States, legislative efforts to control sulfur dioxide and nitrogen dioxide emissions began with the Clean Air Act of 1970. Twenty years later, President George H.W. Bush proposed major changes in the law. The acid rain problem was growing worse, and he felt strongly that stricter controls were needed. In a June 1989 speech, he talked about his commitment to curbing acid rain: "Still, over the last decade, we have not come far enough."[9] In 1990 Congress called for a reduction of 10 million tons (9 million metric tons) of emissions by the year 2010. Similar laws were passed in Canada, as well as in countries of Europe. At a 1994 conference in Oslo, Norway, twelve European nations agreed to reduce sulfur dioxide emissions by nearly 90 percent by 2010.

In February 2002, President George W. Bush proposed a new plan, called the Clear Skies Initiative. It, too, called for sharp reductions of sulfur dioxide and nitrogen oxide emissions. Those reductions would be required by 2018, rather than 2010. In the plan's first phase, more emissions would actually be allowed in the atmosphere, rather than less. Because of that, many environmental scientists believe such a policy would cause the acid rain problem to grow worse. Scientists and politicians continued to debate the plan in 2005.

Cleaner Coal

In accordance with the Clean Air Act, sulfur dioxide and nitrogen oxide emissions must continue to be reduced. Therefore, scientists are developing ways to make fuels cleaner. For instance, coal can be crushed and then sprayed with high-power pressure washers. Then it is sifted through fine screens to remove the dirt and impurities. This method can remove as much as 50 percent of the coal's sulfur content.

Coal can also be cleaned through a process known as **flue gas desulfurization**. These systems are commonly called scrubbers. They cost many millions of dollars, but they are extremely effective. Scrubbers can clean as much as 95 percent of the sulfur from coal before any smoke leaves the chimney. Duke Power, an electric company serving North and South Carolina, has installed coal scrubbers on smokestacks. They are designed to catch smoke and clean it before it goes into the atmosphere. As the coal is burned, sulfur dioxide is created in the chimney flue. The scrubber sprays a mixture of limestone and water onto the gas. A chemical known as calcium sulfate, or gypsum, is formed. The residue falls to the bottom of the scrubber, where it can be collected and recycled in many different ways.

Vehicles of the Future

Scientists are also developing methods to make vehicle engines run cleaner and more efficiently. The catalytic converter is one type of technology that has been installed in cars for about twenty years. This device has proven to reduce the nitrogen oxides released through vehicle exhaust.

Cars built today are more environmentally friendly than older vehicles. Some are designed to use alternative fuels. For instance, General Motors makes pickup trucks that are designed to run on natural gas instead of gasoline. Also, many auto manufacturers are offering vehicles called **hybrids**. These cars, trucks, and sport utility vehicles are designed to run on two or more sources of power, such

The Toyota Prius, a hybrid car that uses both gasoline and electricity, is shown here at a 2005 auto show.

as gasoline and electricity. Their emissions contain a fraction of the nitrogen oxide emitted by gasoline-powered cars, and they are extremely fuel efficient. For instance, the Insight is a hybrid car offered by Honda. It can travel more than 600 miles (966km) on just one tank of gas!

Undoing the Damage

Scrubbing coal and improving transportation can help prevent acid rain in the future. Scientists are

A scientist at a lake in Ontario, Canada, digs up soil samples as part of a long-term study on the effects of acid rain.

also experimenting with ways to treat land that has already been polluted by acids. One of them is Gene E. Likens, who in 1963 became the first person to discover acid rain damage in the United States. Likens has an outdoor laboratory in the White Mountains of New Hampshire called the Hubbard Brook Experimental Forest. Five years ago, he and a team of researchers began spreading calcium over 30 acres (12 hectares) of the forest. Their goal was to replenish nutrients in the soil that had been depleted by acid rain. The experiment worked. Sugar maple seedlings began sprouting all over the treated area. Within two years they were healthier, larger, and greener than seedlings on the untreated land.

Scientists are hopeful about the results of Likens's test. It could pave the way for treatments to other land as well. However, physically adding calcium to the soil is very time consuming and expensive. Although it has potential, it is not a practical way of curing acid damage that affects millions of acres (hectares) of land.

The Past and the Future

With environmental legislation, cleaner coal, better vehicles, and ongoing scientific research, acid rain is less of a problem than it was in the 1970s. Sulfur dioxide emissions in Europe and the United States have dropped significantly. Nitrogen oxide levels have stayed fairly constant, because there are more vehicles on the roads. This, too, will likely improve as cars and trucks become more fuel efficient.

According to Likens, however, governmental efforts are still not keeping up with the damage caused by acid rain. He says that rain in the Northeast is still eight times more acidic than it should be. Still he believes the problem can be solved, and he shares why he is confident that humans will find the answer: "We're a very intelligent species. We got ourselves into this problem, and we know how to get ourselves out."[10]

Notes

Chapter 1: Poisoned Precipitation

1. Michael Allaby, *Fog, Smog & Poisoned Rain*. New York: Facts On File, 2003, pp. 92–93.
2. Allaby, *Fog, Smog & Poisoned Rain*, p. 85.

Chapter 2: Acids in the Clouds

3. Allaby, *Fog, Smog & Poisoned Rain*, p. 90.
4. John V. Miller, "Acid Rain in the Year 2000," New York State Federation of Lake Associations Web Site. www.nysfola.org/acidrain.

Chapter 3: Effects of Acid Rain

5. Quoted in Rujun Shen, "Booming China Awash in 'Out of Control' Acid Rain," *China Digital Times*, November 29, 2004. http://journalism.berkeley.edu/projects/chinadn/en/2004/11/booming_china_a.php.
6. Howard Perlman, "Acid Rain: Do You Need to Start Wearing a Rainhat?" U.S. Geological Survey, *Water Science for Schools*, April 2, 2004. http://ga.water.usgs.gov/edu/acidrain.html.

7. Jim Motavalli, "Death, Be Not Cloud," *Grist Magazine*, September 28, 2004. www.grist.org/ advice/books/2004/09/28/motavalli-cloud.

Chapter 4: Can Acid Rain Be Stopped?

8. Martin Hoffert, telephone interview with the author, May 11, 2004.
9. George H.W. Bush, "Remarks Announcing Proposed Legislation to Amend the Clean Air Act," George Bush Presidential Library, June 12, 1989. http://bushlibrary.tamu.edu/ research/papers/1989/89061201.html.
10. Quoted in Corydon Ireland, "Scientist Sees Hope in Acid Rain Fight," *Democrat and Chronicle*, October 21, 2004. www.democrat andchronicle.com/apps/pbcs.dll/article? AID=/20041021/NEWS01/410210363/-1/ ARCHIVE5.

Glossary

acidic: A term used to describe substances that have a value lower than 7 on the pH scale.

alkalis: Substances that have a value higher than 7 on the pH scale.

carbon dioxide (CO_2): A gas that is created whenever living things breathe and when they die and decompose.

diatoms: Microscopic members of the algae family that live in ponds and other bodies of water.

flue gas desulfurization: A method of scrubbing coal so most of the sulfur dioxide is removed before it gets into the atmosphere.

hybrids: Vehicles that are specially designed to run on both gasoline and electric power.

nitrogen oxide: A gas created when oil and gas products are burned.

pH: A scale that measures a substance's acidity.

sulfur dioxide: A gas created by burning fuels that contain sulfur, most notably coal.

zooplankton: Microscopic organisms that live in water and provide food for aquatic creatures.

For Further Exploration

Books

Alex Edmonds, *Acid Rain*. Mankato, MN: Stargazer Books, 2004. Covers the effects of acid rain on forests and lakes, and includes information on pollution prevention.

Louise Petheram, *Acid Rain*. Mankato, MN: Bridgestone Books, 2002. Discusses the harmful effects that acid rain has on the planet.

Internet Source

MSN Encarta-Acid Rain (http://encarta.msn. com/encyclopedia_761578185/Acid_Rain. html). Provides a very comprehensive explanation of acid rain, including its causes and effects.

Web Sites

EcoKids (www.ecokids.ca). A site by Earth Day Canada that is designed to help inform young people about environmental issues. Includes interactive games, colorful animation, and activities that make learning fun.

The Environmental Literacy Council—For Students (www.enviroliteracy.org/students index.php). An excellent site for anyone who wants to learn more about the environment and the problems it is facing. Includes a section devoted to acid rain, as well as a "Homework Help" section where more information can be found.

Environment Canada—Acid Rain (www.ec. gc.ca/acidrain). An informative, well-written Web site that includes a facts section, case studies, and a special area for students entitled "Kid's Corner."

U.S. Environmental Protection Agency—Acid Rain Students Site (www.epa.gov/acidrain/site_students/index.html). Created especially for young people, this Web site covers what acid rain is, what causes it, why it is harmful, and what is being done to stop it.

U.S. Geological Survey—Water Science for Schools (http://ga.water.usgs.gov/edu/acidrain.html). This Web site explains acid rain's causes and effects. It includes an interesting discussion about rain and what a valuable resource it is.

Index

Picture credits